River Rose

and the Magical Lullaby

Kelly Clarkson

Illustrated by Laura Hughes

First published by HarperCollins Children's Books, a division of HarperCollins Publishers, USA, in 2016
First published in hardback in Great Britain by HarperCollins Children's Books in 2016
First published in paperback in 2017

1 3 5 7 9 10 8 6 4 2

HB ISBN: 978-0-00-821180-6
PB ISBN: 978-0-00-821534-7

HarperCollins Children's Books is a division of HarperCollins Publishers Ltd.

Visit our website at www.harpercollins.co.uk

Printed and bound in China

MIX
Paper from
responsible sources
FSC™ C007454
FSC
www.fsc.org

FSC™ is a non-profit international organisation established to promote
the responsible management of the world's forests. Products carrying the
FSC label are independently certified to assure consumers that they come
from forests that are managed to meet the social, economic and
ecological needs of present and future generations,
and other controlled sources.

Find out more about HarperCollins and the environment at
www.harpercollins.co.uk/green

This book is dedicated to my mother, Jeanne. She taught me the value of education and the thrill of escaping into an adventure by introducing me to the mysteries of the Boxcar Children and the magic of Matilda. She embraced the dreamer in me. May we all be dreamers and never stop believing in magic – just like River Rose.

– K.C.

R iver Rose loves to sing. She loves to make new friends.
She skips and hops, she beeps and bops, she loves to play pretend.

Her best friend's name is Joplin. He loves to dance too.

And tomorrow for the first time, they're going to the zoo!

"Oh, Joplin! I'm so excited. I cannot wait to see
lions that roar and seals that bark –
how long can one night be?"

River Rose tossed and turned. She wouldn't close her eyes
until her mum came in and sang to her this lullaby:

Every night you lie with me.
When I wake you're still here.
I don't know if I ever could find
someone as kind and dear.
No one gets me like you do;
you can tell by my smile.
I'm going to miss you so much while you sleep.
But know that I'm by your side.

A squeaky sound woke River Rose in the middle of the night.

Outside her bedroom window something gave her quite a fright.

She sat up straight and there she saw in front of the shiny moon
a bobbling, wobbling handful of magical balloons!

Soon she was flying and swooshing through the sky
on the adventure of a lifetime, with Joplin by her side.

Then she landed down in the centre of the zoo.

And right round the corner came a bouncy kangaroo.

He was just about to ask if there was something he could do
when River Rose jumped up and said, "We've come to play with you!"

She turned on all the lights and sang, "There's so much I want to see.

Lions, tigers, bears, oh my!... Let's have a zoo party!"

The elephants got things started,
spraying water in the air.
River Rose danced around
and got soaked without a care.

Next she joined the penguins, slipping and sliding in the snow.
The zebras and giraffes joined in and put on quite a show!

Then she asked the turtles, "Can I join you in the water?"

She hopped from pad to pad
and played tag with an otter.
Oh no! A rock below began to
shimmy and to shake.

"Wait! That's not a rock at all!

There's a **hippo** in the lake!"

She saw an ice-cream shop ahead and asked was it okay
to go and build herself an enormous fudge sundae.

River Rose and Joplin continued through the zoo.

She turned and asked her best friend, "What do YOU want to do?"

Joplin took off running right for the merry-go-round.

They rode the ride a hundred times, falling dizzy to the ground.

The polar bears were waiting, playing quietly in the snow.

She asked if she could join them, but they had to let her know,

"We're really all so tired now – polar bears need their sleep.

The trick to fun is to let the day be done.

That's the secret that we keep."

River Rose realised then it was time to say goodbye.
And as the bears snuggled in their den,
she remembered the lullaby:

Every night you lie with me.
When I wake you're still here.
I don't know if I ever could find
someone as kind and dear.

Through the window and then back to bed,
a big smile upon her face.
"That was a great adventure –
but home is my favourite place!"